KU-021-926

DISNEY · PIXAR

Cars

MOVIE THEATER
Storybook

Adapted by Cindy Stierle

Contents

Reader's Digest
Children's Books®

Pleasantville, New York • Montréal, Québec • Bath, United Kingdom

The Rookie

The last car race of the season was about to begin. The winner would take home the biggest prize in racing—the Piston Cup. When the hotshot racer Lightning McQueen rolled onto the racetrack, the crowd roared. McQueen could be the first rookie ever to win the Piston Cup.

Nothing mattered to McQueen except winning.

DISK 1
ROUTE
1

But first McQueen had to beat The King, the legendary racer, who was retiring after this race.

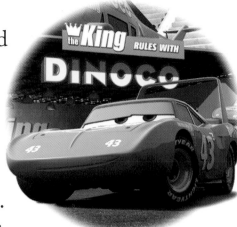

And just as tough to beat was Chick Hicks—a racer who didn't mind playing dirty!

The cars lined up at the starting line, the flag waved, and they were off!

McQueen did some fancy driving, but it was a close race.

To save time, McQueen told his crew not to put on fresh tires when he pulled in for a pit stop. The risky move backfired! KA-BLAM! KA-BLAM—McQueen's rear tires blew out on the last lap!

The King and Chick caught up just as McQueen tried to edge across the finish line. The race was too close to call!

While the judges looked at the instant replay, McQueen told reporters, "I'm a one-man show!" Hearing this, his insulted pit crew quit!

The King tried to offer McQueen some advice. "You ain't gonna win unless you got good folks behind you." But McQueen wasn't listening.

Then the judges announced that the race was a three-way tie. McQueen, The King, and Chick would have a tiebreaking race in California in one week.

McQueen wanted to be the first car to reach California. "We're driving all night," he told Mack, the loyal truck that pulled the trailer McQueen rode in.

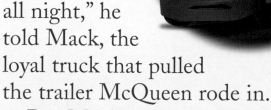

But Mack grew sleepy. When some road pranksters caused him to swerve, a sleeping McQueen rolled out the back of the trailer!

BEEEP! A horn blared, waking McQueen. The confused race car sped off the Interstate looking for

Mack and found himself on old Highway 66. Police lights flashed behind him.

ROUTE 8

A scared McQueen raced away—accidentally tearing up the main street of a small town.

The next morning, McQueen awoke in an impound lot.

DISK 2 ROUTE 9

"Mornin', Sleepin' Beauty," said a rusty tow truck. "My name's Mater."

"What? Where am I?" gasped the very confused McQueen.

"You're in Radiator Springs," Mater said proudly, "the cutest little town in Carburetor County."

It wasn't long before Sheriff arrived. McQueen was due in traffic court.

McQueen didn't think much of the run-down town. And the crowd gathered in the courthouse didn't think much of McQueen—especially the judge, Doc Hudson.

A sleek blue car named Sally was the town attorney. She thought McQueen should fix the road, because

their little town couldn't afford to lose any more business.

So Doc ordered the race car to fix the road before he could leave.

"You gotta be kidding me!" McQueen exclaimed. The rookie wanted to be in California, not in Radiator Springs. But he didn't have a choice. Before long, he was hooked up to a big road-paving machine named Bessie.

McQueen was determined to get
to his big race. He worked fast—
and was sloppy.

"I'm done," McQueen declared.

Doc was angry. "The deal was
you fix the road, not make it worse."

"I'm not a bulldozer, I'm a race
car!" McQueen shot back.

ROUTE
14

"Then why don't we have a little
race. Me and you," Doc challenged.

McQueen could leave if he beat
Doc. But if he lost, he'd have to do
the road over. McQueen smiled.
He thought this was his ticket out
of Radiator Springs.

The entire
town came out
to watch the
race. They
saw the rookie
skid on a sharp
turn and land in
a cactus patch.

Everyone was surprised, except Doc.

"You drive like you fix roads,"
Doc called to the rookie. "Lousy."

Mater laughed as he pulled
McQueen out. "I'm startin' to think he
knowed you was gonna crash."

🔘 *New Friends*

Lightning McQueen worked all night repaving a section of road. In the morning, the townsfolk couldn't believe their eyes—McQueen had done a great job! It looked so good the rest of the town started fixing up their shops, too.

Sally wanted to thank McQueen for his hard work. She invited him to stay in one of the rooms at her motel instead of at the impound lot.

That night, Mater said to McQueen, "I know something we can do." He and McQueen sneaked to a field and went tractor tipping.

Mater crept quietly toward a tractor, and honked his horn. BEEP! The tractor slowly fell over. Then it was McQueen's turn. He revved his engine and the whole field of tractors fell over!

McQueen couldn't believe he was actually having fun! And even though an angry harvester chased them away, the pair had a good laugh— and Mater declared McQueen his new best friend.

The next day Sally invited McQueen for a drive.

"Don't you big city race cars ever just take a drive?" she asked him.

"No, we don't," the surprised McQueen answered. But he followed Sally through the beautiful countryside to a stop overlooking a huge valley.

Sally told him that before the Interstate bypassed the town, Highway 66 had been the main road. "Back then cars didn't drive on it to *make* great time. They drove on it to *have* a great time."

McQueen got another surprise

that day. He learned that Doc was really a legendary race car called the Hudson Hornet who had won three Piston Cups. Doc had been injured in a car wreck. He recovered, but when he returned the racing world had forgotten about him. Doc had been replaced by a hotshot rookie just like McQueen.

ROUTE 5

"Just finish that road and get outta here," Doc told McQueen. He didn't want to have anything to do with a race car.

Once again, McQueen worked all night to finish the road. But getting to the race in California wasn't so important anymore. Instead, he decided to help out his new friends. McQueen became the best customer the town had seen in a long time!

By the end of the day, he looked like a different car.

That night, when the shops turned on their newly repaired neon lights, Radiator Springs looked like a different town!

McQueen had never been happier.

He looked at Sally, wanting to tell her how he felt.

ROUTE 8

DISK 2

ROUTE 9

ROUTE 10

Suddenly, Mack arrived with a swarm of reporters. They had been looking for Lightning McQueen. Before he knew it, McQueen was being whisked away to California. He didn't even get to say good-bye to his new friends.

The townsfolk were sad. They turned off their neon lights and the town was quiet again. Doc stood alone in the center of town—maybe calling the press wasn't such a good idea.

It was finally the day of the big tiebreaking race with The King and Chick. But McQueen didn't care if he won or lost—until he heard a voice on his radio.

"You can win this race with your eyes shut," said Doc. The crowd couldn't believe it. The famous Hudson Hornet was Lightning McQueen's crew chief.

Doc had even pulled a crew together from Radiator Springs. McQueen poured on the speed. He was going to win!

ROUTE 13

The laps ticked by. On the last lap McQueen was in the lead. Then he saw that Chick had caused The King to crash. The rookie stopped. As Chick raced past to win, McQueen turned around and pushed The King across the finish line.

ROUTE 14

ROUTE 15

The fans cheered for McQueen—the rookie who knew what winning really meant.

In Radiator Springs, Sally was back in the mountains that overlooked the town. Suddenly, she heard a voice say, "There's some rumor floating around that some hotshot Piston Cup race car is setting up his big racing headquarters here."

Sally smiled at McQueen. The rookie had never been happier. He had found his home—and himself—in Radiator Springs.

ROUTE 16